A tale of Moominvalley

PUFFIN BOOKS
Published by the Penguin Group: London, New York, Australia,
Canada, India, Ireland, New Zealand and South Africa
Penguin Books Ltd, Registered Offices: 80 Strand, London WC2R 0RL, England

puffinbooks.com

First published 2011
This edition published 2012
001 – 10 9 8 7 6 5 4 3 2 1
Characters and artwork are the original creation of Tove Jansson
Text and illustrations copyright © Moomin Characters™, 2011
Made and printed in China
ISBN: 978-0-141-33059-4

MOOMIN

and the

Moonlight

Adventure

BASED ON THE ORIGINAL STORIES BY

Tove Jansson

PUFFIN

The rain had fallen for days in Moominvalley. But now at last the clouds had cleared and the sun shone down on the Moominhouse.

Moomintroll woke up. He rubbed his eyes and thought a bit.

"Pee-hoo! What a fine day for an adventure!"

"We're going to sail to Lonely Island,"
he announced at breakfast. "We shall go
in search of treasure!"
"Ooh yes," said Snorkmaiden. "I love treasure.
I wonder what I should wear?"

"An adventure, what a good idea," said Moominmamma. "Shall we take a picnic?"

"Why not!" said Moominpappa. "I'd love to do a spot of fishing. I'll get my gear together."

Moomintroll followed Moominpappa out to the shed.

"Shall we take this fishing rod?" said Moomin. "Or this one?"

"Both, I think. Now . . . which hat?" asked Moominpappa. "If there's a storm, I'll need my sou'wester. On the other hand, I'll definitely need my Admiral's hat. And I can't leave my top hat behind . . ."

Moomintroll went to find Moominmamma.
She and Little My were busy picking berries.
   "Pappa and I are all ready for the adventure,"
said Moomintroll excitedly. "Ooh – are you
going to make berry pie?"

"If you like, dear,"
said Moominmamma.

"And I'll make juice," added Little My. "Lots!"
"Yummy!" Moomin said. "I'll go and see if
Snorkmaiden is ready." And off he went.

Snorkmaiden was surrounded by dresses
and beach suits and parasols.
    "This one, or this one, or this one?"
she asked Moomintroll.

"They all look lovely," said Moomintroll.
"But I like the pink one best."
　"Not the blue?" said Snorkmaiden
doubtfully.

*H*ours later, everyone was ready and the boat was piled high with provisions and things they might need.

"At last!" shouted *M*oomintroll.

"We're off to look for treasure!" cried Snorkmaiden.

"But the sun's gone down," said Little My.
   "So it has," said Moominmamma.
"Never mind, we'll have a *moonlight* adventure!"
Everybody cheered.

And so, by the light of the moon,
they sailed away to Lonely Island.

There was a sense of excitement as
the moon shone down on the little boat.

Snorkmaiden looked dreamily down
into the water.
   "Moomintroll," she shouted suddenly.
"Look! There's treasure right below us."

She dipped her hand into the water,
but the treasure slipped away.

"You are silly," said Little My. "That *isn't* treasure, it's just the reflection of the moon!"

"It *is* treasure, real proper treasure," said Snorkmaiden. "Isn't it, Moomintroll?"

"There's only one way to find out," said Moomin . . .

And before anyone could stop him
he dived into the sea.
Down,
down,
down
he swam,
until he reached
the bottom.

In the boat everyone waited anxiously. Snorkmaiden felt awful. She really wanted the treasure but she also wanted Moomintroll back safe and sound.

But then, suddenly, there he was at the side of the boat.

"There *was* treasure," said Moomintroll, "and the moon showed me where to find it."
He handed Snorkmaiden a beautiful shell with a pearl the colour of the moon nestled inside.

By the time they reached the island, everyone was still talking about Moomin's big adventure.

"You must be hungry, my little Moomintroll," said Moominmamma. "I think it's time for a moonlight picnic!"

So they all sat around the campfire, laughing and singing and listening to Moominpappa's tales of his exploits at sea.

Then the stars started to fade
                  and it was time to get some rest.

Snorkmaiden leaned her head on Moomintroll's shoulder. "Thank you for fetching the treasure for me," she said sleepily. "You were very brave."

"I'll find you even more tomorrow,"
said Moomin proudly, "because I think it
may be another fine day for an adventure."
And with that, they fell fast asleep.

The End